The Importance of Being 3

BY Lindsay Ward

SCHOLASTIC INC.

For Frank, always

ISBN 978-1-338-16402-2

Text and art copyright © 2016 by Lindsay Ward. All rights reserved. Published by Scholastic Inc., 557 Broadway, New York, NY 10012, by arrangement with Dial Books for Young Readers, an imprint of Penguin Young Readers Group, a division of Penguin Random House LLC. SCHOLASTIC and associated logos are trademarks and/or registered trademarks of Scholastic Inc.

12 11 10 9 8 7 6 5 4 3 2   17 18 19 20 21 22

Printed in the U.S.A.   40

First Scholastic printing, January 2017

Designed by Mina Chung
Text set in Chaloops
This art was created using cut paper, ink, and pencil.

All the best things
come in three.

Not **1** or **2** but **3**

Three bears,

three pigs.

Three kittens, too!

I'm writing letters.

I'm learning
what it means to share.

Give it back!

Look over here.
See what I drew?

A special shape
with three sides, too!

Play outside,

new things to do.

KICK

THROW

CATCH

I've learned so much

since I was two.

THIRD STREET PRESCHOOL

I have important places to be.

A brand-new bike
just for me.

Three big wheels.
I'll race you there.
To the corner and back,

TRIPLE-DOG
DARE!

Visit the park.

Hop,

swing,

and slide.

Play with friends.

Count 1, 2, 3... HIDE!

POOL

Afternoon swim.
Dad comes, too.

Ready,
set, go!

Try something new.

Pull on my swimmies.
Practice my kicks.

Motorboat bubbles.
See my new tricks.

On the way home
grab something sweet.
Neapolitan,
my favorite treat!

Then just like that,
I pout and snap!

Looks like someone
needs a nap.

My mom begins
to count to THREE.

TOTAL

MELTDOWN

Uh-oh! Time-out.
She points at me.

MODE

I throw a fit.
Some days are rough.
I cry and scream.
Three sure is tough.

My mom comes in.
Big tight hug.
Time-out's over.

I LOVE YOU, BUG.

No more tears.

The grumps are gone.

Here come my friends.

Let's go, come on!

Let's play pretend.

ROAR.

I cry.

Lions, tigers,
and bears. Oh my!

Sit down for dinner.

Table for three.

Oops! Big spill all over me.

Time for bubbles.
Jump in the tub.

Three yellow duckies.
Rub-a-dub-dub.

Footie pajamas!
Ready for bed.

Grab three books,
to fill my head.